There Is No Othe !

SYLVIA J. FOUST
Illustrator: Brian Rivera

WestBow Press books may be ordered through booksellers or by contacting:

WestBow Press
A Division of Thomas Nelson & Zondervan
1663 Liberty Drive
Bloomington, IN 47403
www.westbowpress.com
844-714-3454

Illustrated by Brian Rivera

Scripture taken from the World English Bible.

ISBN: 978-1-6642-3794-0 (sc)
ISBN: 978-1-6642-3796-4 (hc)
ISBN: 978-1-6642-3795-7 (e)

Library of Congress Control Number: 2021912486

Print information available on the last page.

WestBow Press rev. date: 06/25/2021

WESTBOW
PRESS®
A DIVISION OF THOMAS NELSON
& ZONDERVAN

Dedicated to God's plan. May he use this book as he sees fit to encourage his children of all ages.

For my grandchildren Liam, Emilia, Olivia, Douglas and Thomas who inspired this book with their questions and unique personalities. I love you all forever and a day.

Thank you Tom for your amazing love and support.

Thank you Annie for your friendship and encouragement.

"May Yahweh bless you and keep you. May Yahweh make his face shine on you, and be gracious to you. May Yahweh lift up his face toward you, and give you peace."

AMEN

Numbers 6: 24-26

BILLIONS of people.
It's a big world out there.
But there is no other YOU.
If you looked everywhere.

You might have big hair.
Or no hair at all.
Are your eyes blue or green?
Or brown like the fall?

You might be athletic.
Or really like art.
How about arithmetic?
Or making things start?

You might be a tall one.
Or be very petite.
Do you like to eat lemons?
Or only like sweets?

You might really love ice cream.
In a cone or a cup.
You might like asparagus.
Or you might throw it up.

You might like to daydream.
Or stick to the facts.
You might like to grow things.
Or love wearing hats.

You might like big boats.
Or prefer the dry land.
You might like green meadows.
Or playing in the sand.

You might love big dogs.
Or REALLY big cats.
You might love all animals.
Or only like bats.

You might like soft music.
Or dance to a beat.
You might dance on your toes.
Or have two left feet.

You might dream of space.
Or diving deep in the sea.
Whatever you dream of.
That is what you can be!

We all have emotions.
Like joy, fear, or sadness.
Do your best to be kind.
And you'll like what happens.

When you are in a tough spot,
you're not sure what to do.
It helps to remember
just how much God loves YOU!

FEELINGS

HAPPY

BORED

ANGRY

SORRY

PLAYFUL

HOPEFUL

PROUD

SAD

SCARED

It is how you are different.
That will help you go far.
You have gifts like no other.
Only you set the bar.

So, no matter your appearance.
Or emotions you feel.
You just need to know that
God's love is for real.

THERE IS NO OTHER YOU!
You are one of a kind.
God's perfect creation.
His perfect design.

Psalm 139: 13-14

For you formed my inmost being.
You knit me together in my mother's womb.

I will give thanks to you, for I am fearfully and wonderfully
made. Your works are wonderful.
My soul knows that very well.

Jeremiah 29:11

"For I know the thoughts that I think toward you," say's
Yahweh, "thoughts of peace, and not of evil, to give you
hope and a future."

Isaiah 40:29-31

He gives power to the weak.
He increases the strength of him who has no might. Even
the youths faint and get weary, and the young men utterly
fall; but those who wait for Yahweh will renew their strength.

They will mount up with wings like eagles.
They will run, and not be weary.
They will walk, and not faint.

World English Bible

Things to talk about:

Do you know what it feels like to be made fun of?

Have you ever felt sad because of things people have said about you?

What is the thing you like most about yourself and why?

Can God use your favorite thing to help others?

What is something you don't like about yourself and why?

Can you change what you don't like, and do you really need to?

Can God help you to be happy when things aren't great?

How can you encourage others who might feel bad about themselves?

Do you believe that God made you just the way you are for a reason?

Do you thank God every day for all of the good things in your life and ask him to help you when you are sad?

"May Yahweh bless you and keep you. May Yahweh make his face to shine on you, and be gracious to you. May Yahweh lift up his face toward you, And give you peace."

AMEN

Numbers 6: 24-26

THERE IS NO OTHER YOU!

Lightning Source UK Ltd.
Milton Keynes UK
UKHW050940190721
387390UK00006B/14

9 781664 237940